T5-CVE-912

JOURNEYS

L Le 88

JOURNEYS

The Adventures of Leaf

Louann Carroll

1992
Weasel Books
P.O. Box 65611, St. Paul, Minnesota 55165, U.S.A.

Journeys. © Copyright 1992 by Louann Carroll. All rights reserved. Printed in the United States of America. No part of this book may be used or reproduced in any manner whatsoever without written permission from the publisher except in the case of brief quotations embodied in critical articles and reviews.

FIRST EDITION

Art by the students of Timothy E. Doyle, Centerville Junior High School, Fremont, California

ISBN 1-880090-03-1

 Printed on recycled paper

Weasel Books are published by
Galde Press, Inc.
P.O. Box 65611
St. Paul, Minnesota 55165

*Dedicated to
Shannon,
Dennis
& Ryan*

*and to Phyllis,
who believed in
the story.*

The Separation

Blue skies and sunshine shone down upon the forest floor. The wind blew softly through the pines, showering the Earth with the soft sound of pine needles. Alone against a rock jutting out from the side of a mountain grew one small maple tree. All of the leaves had blown off into the wind save one. Her name was Leaf and she grew out from Twig. Both Leaf and Twig were not terribly old as they had both burst forth in late summer.

"Oh, Twig," Leaf shouted loudly. "What a beautiful day! Twig, wake up!"

Eric Aldridge

"Be quiet, Leaf. I am trying to sleep," Twig mumbled grouchily. "Leave me alone."

"But you have to wake up. I feel something in the air, something exciting and wonderful," Leaf remarked nervously. "I just know it. As a matter of fact I feel decidedly different this morning. You know? Sort of like there's a part of me missing. Kind of half there, if you know what I mean."

"Leaf. Leaf. Leaf. You can exaggerate. How can anyone be half there and half not? Silly talk is what it is. Just plain silly," Twig replied irritably. "Now let me sleep."

"I understand what you are saying Twig," Leaf replied while flipping her body into a passing breeze. "But it does not change one thing. I am half here, and if you would just wake up you would notice it too."

L.E.M. 88

Twig managed to wake up enough to reach around inside himself feeling for the special place that connected Twig with Leaf. When he became aware of it, he found that indeed half of them was no longer connected.

"What have you gone and done, Leaf?" Twig shouted. "I knew you would eventually go and do something stupid. Just how could you do this?"

"Wait, Twig. Please wait," Leaf pleaded. "I didn't do this thing. It was not done by me! This is what must have happened to all the other leaves. Oh dear, I was so foolish as to think it could never happen to us."

"Be quiet, Leaf," Twig demanded. "I must think. Please be patient a moment."

Quietly they clung to the tree, the two of them. Not as sure of themselves as they had once been, never dreaming that they would ever be parted—least of all by something beyond their nature to understand.

The wind began to rise, blowing ever more strongly with each passing moment.

After a while Leaf began to whisper quietly to Twig. "Twig, I know you will be angry. But I believe that this is the right thing to do. I am not sure exactly why, but it is right, Twig. I just know it."

"How can you say that to me, Leaf?" Twig shook angrily. "We are one. Not two, as you would have us be."

"It doesn't matter how we feel," Leaf tried to say gently. "I know that it is no longer possible for us to be one."

Use this page to create your own picture of Leaf on her adventures.

Weeping silently, she turned away. "From now on Twig, we shall be two."

At that moment the wind grew to a monstrous roar and the trees of the forest gave up their last leaves. For one last moment Leaf and Twig were one; the next, two.

Serina Lucero 88

The Thornbush

"Come back, Leaf," Twig pleaded. "Please, Leaf, please come back. Don't leave me here alone."

But Twig was left crying into the wind.

Flying as if on a roller coaster, up and down, through pine trees and fir trees, around huge boulders and gulleys.

"Oh my !" Leaf shouted up into the Wind. "What a marvelous ride. I don't think I would ever wish it to stop. I will ride on forever. Never caring, never wanting, just flying forever."

Anju Kumar

"Be careful little Leaf," the Wind warned her. "One must always watch where one is going, or they may not like where they end up."

"Don't be silly, Wind," Leaf shouted up at her. "Why should I care where it is as long as I am riding the wind?"

Suddenly Leaf screamed in agony. For the moment she was blinded by the pain that seemed to pierce her middle. From somewhere around her came a huge thorn that had shoved itself right through her. She began to feel the stirrings of panic and soon lost all thought of herself in her struggle for survival.

Much later, when the first panic had subsided, she glanced around and found herself stuck right in the center of what appeared to be a gigantic thornbush.

"What have I done?" moaned Leaf as she turned and noticed that her middle had begun to turn brown. "I am changing, I will never be the same. Now Twig will not know me when I return."

"Be quiet, little Leaf," the Thornbush rustled softly. "We all change, yet still remain the same. Calm yourself and, with the help of the Wind, we will get you down."

With her leaves glistening brightly in the Sun and her thorns glinting dangerously, she called out to the Wind to come to the aid of Leaf.

The Thornbush bent into the breeze, and with a twist of her thorn and the help of the Wind, Leaf was soon drifting softly to the ground.

Leaf breathed a sigh of relief as the Earth slowly came up to greet her. She nestled into the dirt and welcomed the cushioning of the Thornbush's autumn-dropped leaves.

"Oh thank you," Leaf whispered. "It doesn't seem so painful now, and I think if I just rest here a while I will be ready to resume my journey. You don't mind if I rest here, do you?" she asked.

"Of course I do not mind," Thornbush answered. "You may stay as long as you like."

"However," Thornbush asked thoughtfully, "just what did you think you were doing?"

"I really don't think it is any of your business," Leaf answered haughtily.

"I saved your life, little Leaf," replied Thornbush, "and that makes it my business."

Thornbush looked searchingly at Leaf and went on, "If you do not learn from your mistakes, Little One, you will be doomed to repeat them."

"None of this, "Leaf said softly, "was any of my fault. I relied on the Wind to take care of me. After all, that is her job. She took me from Twig. She made me take this Journey. She threw me into your thorn. It is her fault that now I am changed and Twig will not recognize me."

"Little Leaf," Thornbush instructed, "it is your nature, being a Leaf, to experience a Journey. Journeys are something all leaves must take. However, you chose to be tossed about in the Wind with no mind to where you might be going. That choice is what brought you here today."

Draw your picture of Leaf and Thornbush on this page.

"So," continued Thornbush, "Although you may not like it, you have no one to blame but your own ignorance, and that is where I come in. You must always remember, never blame another for your own mistakes."

Leaf, unwilling to accept responsibility, hugged to herself the comforting thought that of course the Thornbush was somehow misguided.

Leaf was sure that she knew who was to blame.

Suddenly, from all around her Leaf heard laughter. Much to her surprise, the leaves, some of which she was lying on, were laughing at her.

"Silly Leaf," one of the leaves remarked.

"Must be rather young," another one giggled.

"Dumb leaves," Leaf thought to herself. "They have no idea how hard Journeying is."

Then Leaf remembered the Thornbush's words. "Journeys are something all leaves must take."

"Excuse me," Leaf said to one rather brown, withered leaf. "Have you ever gone on a Journey?"

"Of course I have, little Leaf. Is this your first one?" asked withered Leaf.

"Yes," Leaf replied. "And I am completely unsure as to what to do next. The Thornbush says so much, but her words mean little to me. Can you tell me what it is I should do next?"

"No, Leaf, I can't. Every Journey is different for every Leaf. For every Leaf sees and experiences life differently. But, I can tell you, Leaf. You are never alone."

"Everyone speaks so strangely around here," Leaf thought to herself. And with that she drifted off to sleep.

M.J. Kelly

Morning comes slowly to the forest in the fall, starting first with the song of the birds and following with the Sun's first beams reaching the pine fresh floor.

As the gentle rays hit upon the little Leaf, she reached around inside herself to find out just how much damage had been done.

The hole in her middle did not seem to be so bad as first thought. The edges had grown quite brown but she felt reasonably well and ready to resume her Journey.

Her friend the Wind was just a tiny breeze this morning. Leaf found to her delight that if she moved just so, bending her stem this way and that, she could determine just which way she could want to fly.

The hole in her middle helped to slow her down some so that she didn't rush headlong in any direction so fast that she could not see.

Nicole Bodily "88"

"Look, Thornbush," Leaf cried excitedly. "I can go where I choose! I can go left and I can go right or even up and down if I want."

At that moment she tugged a bit too much on her stem and landed headfirst into Thornbush's trunk.

"Well," Leaf said, a bit stunned, "I suppose I could use a little bit of practice. But I know if I try, I can do it!"

"Certainly you can, little Leaf," rustled the Thornbush. "You are the one in control, and with the help of the Wind you may go where you want. You are at the mercy of no one, and you are never alone."

"I see. Yes, I really do see now," Leaf replied thoughtfully. "I was so busy enjoying the ride I did not care what might happen or where I might end up. But, I suppose, like most leaves I had to learn it on my own."

After all," Leaf mused, "a lesson learned well is one never forgotten."

"So now you have," Thornbush said. "Now it is time for you to resume your Journey."

"Good-bye, Thornbush. I will not forget you. Thank you ever so much for your help and kindness."

With a twitch of her stem and a call to the Wind, Leaf was again on her way.

Freedom to Choose

Brightly bounding through the skies, Leaf practiced twitching her stem, moving her in new directions. Swirling round and round, she learned how to land and how to fly again. Leaf loved the feel of the wind beneath her and reveled in her newfound freedom of motion.

Sometimes she would stop at night just to start again first thing in the morning. Sometimes she would not stop at all.

"Heavens!" Leaf cried out loud. "What can that be?"

"That is Water," moaned the Wind.

"I must stop and see it or I will fall apart!" Leaf cried dramatically. "I have never seen such beauty!"

The water shone brilliantly in the warm October Sun, creating sparkles of light and nearly blinding Leaf's view of it.

The forest reached down to the water's edge, and from Leaf's height it seemed as perfect as new-blown glass.

"But, dear Leaf, water is not for leaves. Alas, beautiful as it is, it is not for you," Wind sighed gently.

"Bother," Leaf replied. "I will decide what is not for me. I say it is and I will go where I please."

With a swish of her stem and a downward motion, Leaf headed for the sparkling beauty below her.

Upon closer inspection of the water, Leaf soon realized that it was not so solid as first appearance suggested.

As a matter of fact, it seemed to move in a somewhat fluid motion and, before she could stop her downward flight, she ended up right in the middle of it.

"What have I done now?" Leaf screeched. "I think I am sinking. I am going right to the bottom. Help! Someone help!"

"Hello there, Leaf," the Water lapped. "How did you manage to get yourself here? Everyone knows," Water babbled, "Leaves and Water do not mix."

"I know, I know," muttered Leaf. "The Wind tried to tell me. But again, I would not listen. I think that perhaps I need to learn things on my own, even if I do end up getting hurt. Otherwise how do I know if what I hear is the truth? But none of this matters now if I die. Can you help me, please?"

"I can," said the Water. "But most importantly, I will. You see, it is my choice to help you."

"You do talk rather silly, you know," Leaf replied. "Please tell me what I should do and I will do it."

Leaf snickered, "By my choice, you see."

"Do nothing but lie still, Leaf. I will carry you on the back of my waves and soon I will have you deposited safely upon the shore," a dignified Water retorted.

Leaf, floating patiently, waited for the wave. She was still a bit uneasy, feeling herself helpless to the fancy of the Water.

"I will never do this to myself again. From now on I will be more careful. Why does Journeying take so much out of oneself? Learning is not easy, not not easy at all," Leaf thought.

"Hold on, Leaf," shouted Water. "We are coming!"

With a bump, a wave hit Leaf, and for a moment she thought she would go down altogether. But it only served to give her a forward motion, and she could feel the touch of her friend Wind on her back.

Shortly she found herself near shore. With a flick of her water-sodden stem and a quick breath of Wind, she lay wet and miserable on the shore of her beautiful lake.

"Thank you, Water, and you too, Wind. I seem to get myself out of one problem, then throw myself into another. At this rate I'll never get any rest. Could you, for the moment, leave me please?" Leaf wearily asked. "I am sorely disappointed in myself and I need time to think this all through."

As she lay in the Sun, Leaf could feel her body begin to dry, curling slightly around the edges. Uncomfortable still, and angry, she questioned the reason for her Journey.

"There is no chance now that Twig would ever recognize me. I have turned quite brown and feel very old and stiff. There seem to be cracks showing through my body, and I can see that this Journey will lead to my end."

"Me," thought Leaf, "who thought there could never be an end. My life. Gone. Forever. Journeys are for dying."

"Oh, my dear little Leaf," whispered the Wind. "Everything dies. You. Me. The trees. Why, even Water will dry up someday. Death is a part of life. How could anyone know the beauty of living without the agony of dying? They are only the tools with which to gauge your experiences.

"But enough of this," said Wind. "You certainly have time for another trip with me before you decide to wither away. Come now! Life was not meant to worry about death, for death was given to us so we could appreciate life!"

"I see your point, Wind," Leaf replied. "I will come for one more ride. I feel as if I might make it, but pieces of me are already breaking away. I think it might have to be a short one, but thank you for asking."

Use this page to show Leaf's last ride with Wind.

New Beginnings

Leaf could barely bend in the wind, so brown and still was her body. As she flew, more and more pieces of her began to chip away until there was barely enough left of her to keep her floating.

But Leaf, being Leaf, loved every moment.

"Oh Wind, thank you ever so much for this last ride. I will miss you greatly," Leaf sorrowed.

Wind swept down and sent her flying joyously into the air.

"I will never forget you for this. Perhaps we may even meet again one day. The only thing I do regret is that I have not learned and loved more."

"Remember this, Leaf," the Wind moaned while sending her into a tailspin. "We only learn little bits at a time. There is only so much we can learn in one lifetime, however long or short it may be. You can only try to do your best. That is all that can be asked."

Leaf soared downward.

"Goodbye, Leaf. Goodbye," shouted the Wind. "Until we meet again."

Leaf spun crazily in the air before coming to rest beneath a tiny tree.

"Wait, Wind!" she pleaded. "There is something I must say. Please wait!"

But it was too late, for Wind had already gone.

"I love you Wind," Leaf said to herself. "Perhaps I have loved greatly after all."

The warm October air had turned into November's chill, and Leaf lay on the ground, a mere skeleton of her former self.

As she gazed into the cold, gray winter sky, she recognized the small maple where she had begun.

"Up there, somewhere, is Twig," she mourned. "He knows nothing of my being here."

"I loved you too, Twig. I loved you very much. I have learned and loved and sorrowed as much as I could have," Leaf thought to herself, "and that is as it should be. I suppose that is what my nature intended it to be."

November's chill brought December's bitter snow. Leaf was buried beneath the great white drifts. She no longer thought much of herself, as there was not much left of her to think of.

The last thing she remembered was the quiet, dark and musty smell of the damp earth beneath her.

Spring came early that year. The snow turned into rain, in the blink of an eye it seemed.

The cold season was over and the Sun shone once again on the forest. The smell of the rich, warm soil permeated the air.

New buds formed on the small maple tree, and from somewhere deep down into the Earth, the tree's roots pulled in the essence of what was once Leaf and hurled her into a small, brown twig where a tiny, green bud formed.

Startled, an older and wiser Twig looked down with surprise at the tiny, green bud. Slowly and gently, the bud unfurled its leaves, and Twig remembered Leaf with love.

Preparing herself for what was sure to be more pain, Twig turned and felt for that special place that joined Twig and Leaf.

Suddenly she felt a sudden rush of love course through her. "I am alive!"

And the Journey begins again.

Sandy Rego 88

Use these blank pages to draw your own adventures of Leaf.